THE STORY OF
DOCTOR DOLITTLE

THE STORY OF
DOCTOR DOLITTLE

Being the History of His Peculiar Life at Home and
Astonishing Adventures in Foreign Parts.
Never Before Printed.

TOLD AND ILLUSTRATED BY
HUGH LOFTING

ADAPTED FOR YOUNGER READERS
BY N. H. KLEINBAUM

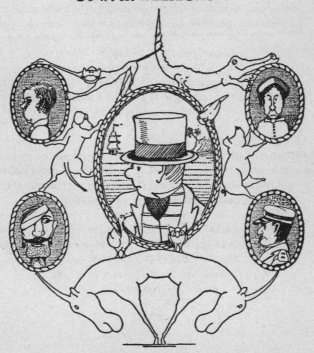

A YEARLING BOOK

Published by
Bantam Doubleday Dell Books for Young Readers
a division of
Bantam Doubleday Dell Publishing Group, Inc.
1540 Broadway
New York, New York 10036

The trademarks Yearling® and Dell® are registered in the
U.S. Patent and Trademark Office and in other countries.
ISBN: 0-440-41233-1
Printed in the United States of America
March 1997
10 9 8 7 6 5
CWO

TO ALL CHILDREN
CHILDREN IN YEARS AND
CHILDREN IN HEART
I DEDICATE THIS STORY

CONTENTS

THE STORY OF
DOCTOR DOLITTLE

PUDDLEBY

Once upon a time, there was a doctor named John Dolittle, M.D. He lived in a little town called Puddleby-on-the-Marsh. Whenever he walked down the street in his high hat the people would say, "There goes the Doctor! What a clever man!"

Dogs and children followed him. The house he lived in was very small but had a large garden with a wide lawn, stone seats and weeping willow trees. His sister, Sarah, took care of the house for him. The Doctor looked after the garden.

Doctor Dolittle loved animals and had many kinds of pets. There were goldfish in the pond, rabbits in the pantry, white mice in his piano, a squirrel in the linen closet and a hedgehog in the cellar. He also had a cow and a calf and an old, lame horse. But of all of them, the Doctor's favorite pets were Dab-Dab, the duck; Jip, the dog; Gub-Gub, the baby pig; Polynesia, the parrot; and Too-Too, the owl.

Sarah grumbled about all the animals. She said they made the house a mess. One day, an old lady with rheumatism came to see the Doctor and sat on the hedgehog, who was sleeping on the sofa. The old lady was so scared she never came to Doctor Dolittle again!

Sarah was angry and said, "John, how can you expect sick people to come and see you when you keep all these animals in the house? If you go on like this, no one will come to see you!"

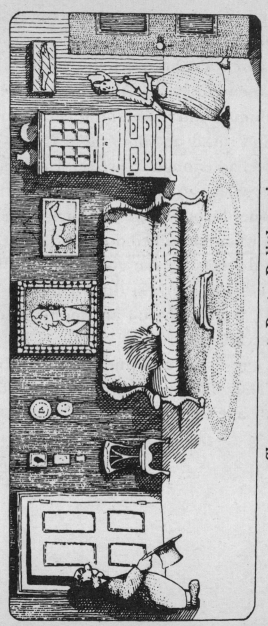

She never came to Doctor Dolittle again.

"But I like the animals," Doctor Dolittle said with a frown.

"You are ridiculous," Sarah snorted.

As time went by, the Doctor saw more and more animals and fewer and fewer people. If he hadn't saved up some money, he would not have had enough to live on. He kept getting more pets, and it cost a lot to feed them. The money he had saved was quickly used up.

Now when he walked down the street people would say, "There goes John Dolittle, M.D.! He was the best doctor in the West Country. Now he hasn't any money and his stockings are full of holes!"

But the dogs, cats and children didn't mind. They still followed him through town, the same as when he was rich.

ANIMAL LANGUAGE

I t happened one day that the Doctor was talking with the cat's-meat man, who had come to see the Doctor because he had a stomachache.

"Why don't you give up being a people's doctor and be an animal doctor?" the cat's-meat man asked Doctor Dolittle.

Polynesia, the parrot, was sitting in the window, singing a sailor song to herself. She stopped singing and listened.

"You see, Doctor," the cat's-meat man said,

"Be an animal doctor."

"you know more about animals than the vets do. The book you wrote about cats was wonderful! You know the way cats think. You can make money doctoring animals, too. Be an animal doctor."

When the cat's-meat man had left, the parrot flew to the Doctor's table. "That man's got sense," she said. "That's what you should do. Be an animal doctor."

"But there are plenty of animal doctors," John Dolittle said as he put some flowerpots outside to catch the rain.

"But none of them are any good," said Polynesia. "Now listen. Did you know that animals can talk?"

"I know that parrots can talk," said the doctor.

"We can talk in two languages—people's language and bird language," she said proudly. "If I say 'Polly wants a cracker,' you understand me. But listen to this: Ka-ka oi-ee, fee-fee?"

"What does that mean?" cried the Doctor.

"That means 'Is the porridge hot yet?' in bird language."

"You don't say," said the Doctor, scratching his head. "You never talked to me that way before."

"Why should I?" said Polynesia. "You wouldn't have understood."

"Tell me some more," said the Doctor, getting excited. He rushed to get a notebook and a pencil. "Now, don't go too fast. I'll write this down. This is very interesting. First, give me the birds' ABC, but go slowly."

And that was how Doctor Dolittle learned that animals had languages and could talk to one another. All that afternoon, Polynesia sat on the kitchen table, giving him bird words to add to his book.

At teatime, Jip, the dog, came in. "See, he's talking to you," the parrot said to Doctor Dolittle.

"It looks like he's scratching his ear."

"Animals don't always speak with their mouths," Polynesia said. "They talk with their bodies—their ears, feet, and tails. See how he's twitching up one side of his nose?"

"What does that mean?"

"That means 'Can't you see that it has stopped raining?'" Polynesia explained. "Dogs use their noses to ask questions."

With Polynesia's help, the Doctor learned the languages of the animals so well that he could talk to them himself and understand everything they said. That's when he gave up being a people's doctor.

The cat's-meat man told everyone that John Dolittle was now only an animal doctor. Old ladies brought their pet pugs and poodles. Farmers came with their sick cows and sheep.

As soon as the other animals found that Doctor Dolittle could speak their language, they told him where the pain was or what bothered them and it was easy for him to cure them.

In a few years, every living thing heard about John Dolittle, M.D. The birds who flew to other countries in the winter told animals in foreign lands of Doctor Dolittle.

That is how he became famous among all the animals of the world.

MORE MONEY TROUBLES

And soon the doctor began to make money again. His sister, Sarah, bought a new dress and was happy.

Some of the animals who came to see Doctor Dolittle were so sick that they stayed for a week. When they were getting better, they sat in chairs on the lawn. Even after they got well, many did not want to leave. The Doctor always let them stay.

Once, when Doctor Dolittle was sitting on his garden wall in the evening, an organ-

They sat in chairs on the lawn.

grinder came by with a monkey tied to a string. The Doctor saw that the collar was tight around the monkey's neck. The monkey looked very unhappy. Doctor Dolittle took the monkey from the man, gave him a shilling, and told him to go away.

The man yelled angrily, but the Doctor took the monkey into his house and closed the door. The other animals in the house called the monkey Chee-Chee, which means "ginger" in monkey language.

When the circus came to town, a crocodile with a bad toothache escaped and came to the Doctor's garden. The Doctor talked to him in crocodile language and made his tooth better. When the crocodile saw how nice the house was, he asked if he could stay. He asked if he could sleep in the fishpond at the bottom of the garden, and promised he would not eat any fish.

But because of the crocodile, old ladies were afraid to send their lapdogs to Doctor Dolittle. Farmers thought he would eat their sick lambs and calves.

The crocodile upset Sarah Dolittle very much.

"John!" she cried. "You must send that creature away! This is the last straw. I will no longer keep house for you if you don't send away that alligator."

"It isn't an alligator, it's a crocodile," the Doctor said.

"No matter," Sarah huffed. "It's a nasty thing to find under the bed. I won't have it in this house."

"But he has promised he will not bite anyone," the Doctor answered. "He doesn't like the circus. I haven't the money to send him to his home in Africa."

"I tell you, I *will not* have him around," said Sarah. "If you don't send him away I'll . . . I'll go and get married!"

The Doctor looked at his angry sister and shrugged. "Then go and get married. It can't be helped."

Sarah packed her things and quickly left. The Doctor was alone with his animal family.

He was poorer than he had ever been before. But the Doctor refused to worry.

"Money is a nuisance," he said. "We'd all be much better off if it had never been invented. Who cares about money as long as we are happy?"

But soon even the animals began to worry. One night, as the Doctor snored in his chair before the kitchen fire, they whispered among themselves about what to do.

The owl, Too-Too, who was good at arithmetic, figured that there was only enough money to last one week—if they each had only one meal a day.

"I think we should do the housework ourselves," Polynesia suggested. "After all, it's because of us that the Doctor is so lonely and poor."

They agreed that Chee-Chee, the monkey,

would do the cooking and mending; Jip, the dog, would sweep the floors; Dab-Dab, the duck, would dust and make the beds; Too-Too, the owl, would keep the accounts; and Gub-Gub, the pig, would do the gardening. Because she was the oldest, Polynesia, the parrot, would be housekeeper and laundress.

At first the new jobs were very hard to do—except for Chee-Chee, who had hands and could do things like a person. But soon they got used to it and thought it was great fun to watch Jip sweep his tail over the floor with a rag tied to it for a broom. They worked so well that the Doctor said his house had never been so clean before!

The animals built a vegetable and flower stall outside the garden gate. They sold radishes and roses to people going by on the road.

But there still was not enough money to pay the bills. Yet Doctor Dolittle did not worry.

"Never mind," he said. "The hens lay eggs and the cow gives milk. We can always have omelets and pudding. There are plenty of vegetables in the garden. The winter is a long way off."

But that year the snow came earlier than usual. Although the horse hauled in lots of wood from the forest for big fires in the kitchen, most of the vegetables were gone. For the first time, the animals were really hungry.

A MESSAGE FROM AFRICA

That winter was very cold. One night in December, sitting around the warm kitchen fire, the doctor read aloud from books he had written in animal language. Suddenly Too-Too, the owl, said, "Shhh! What's that noise outside?"

They listened. Someone was running outside. The door flew open. Chee-Chee ran in, gasping for breath.

"Doctor," he cried, "I've just had a message from my cousin in Africa. Hundreds of monkeys there have come down with a terrible sickness. They've heard of you and beg you to come to Africa to help!"

"Who brought the message?" asked the Doctor.

"A swallow. She is outside on the rain-spout," Chee-Chee said.

"Bring her in by the fire before she catches cold!"

The swallow came in, frightened, huddled and shivering. Soon she warmed up and sat on the mantelpiece, telling the Doctor of the terrible sickness.

"I would gladly go to Africa," the Doctor said, "especially in this cold weather. But we don't have enough money to buy the tickets." The Doctor was quiet for a moment. "I helped a sailor's baby get well from the measles once. Maybe he'll lend us his boat to go to Africa, since this is an emergency."

Early the next morning, the Doctor went to the seashore. He returned and told the animals the sailor would lend them the boat and they could leave for Africa.

The crocodile, the monkey and the parrot were very glad. They sang for joy to be going back to Africa, their real home.

"I will only be able to take you three—with Jip, Dab-Dab, Gub-Gub, and Too-Too," the Doctor said. "The rest of the animals will have to go live in the fields where they were born until we come home. Most of them sleep through the winter, so they won't mind."

Polynesia, who had been on many long sea voyages in her lifetime, told the Doctor all they would need on the ship.

"You must have plenty of bread—hardtack, they call it," she said. "And you must have beef in cans and an anchor."

"I expect the ship will have its own anchor," said the Doctor.

"Well, make sure," said Polynesia. "It's very important. You can't stop if you don't have an anchor."

The Doctor looked at the list. "Where are we going to get the money for this?" he asked. "Oh, bother! Money again! I'll ask the grocer if he'll wait for his money until I get back. I'll send the sailor to ask him."

So the sailor went to the grocer. Soon he came back with all the things they needed.

The animals quickly packed up. They closed the house and gave the key to the old horse, who lived in the stable. They made sure there was plenty of hay in the loft to last the horse through the winter. Then they carried their things to the seashore.

As soon as they were on the ship, Gub-Gub, the pig, asked where the beds were. He was ready for his four o'clock nap. Polynesia took him downstairs inside the ship. She showed him the beds. They were set on top of each other like bookshelves.

"That isn't a bed!" cried Gub-Gub. "That's a shelf!"

"Beds are like that on ships," said the parrot. "It's called a bunk. Climb up and go to sleep."

Gub-Gub changed his mind. "I'm too excited to sleep. I want to go upstairs."

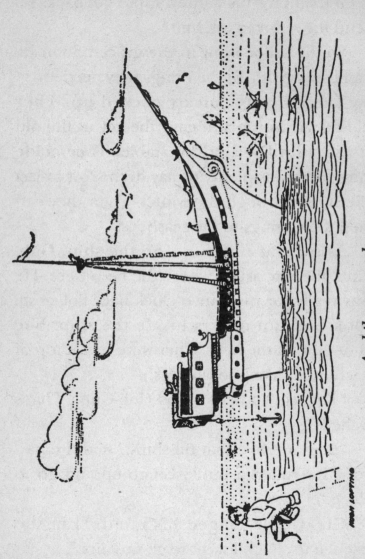

And the voyage began.

"Well, this *is* your first trip," Polynesia said. "You'll get used to it after a while."

They were about to start the journey when the Doctor said he had to go back to ask the sailor how to get to Africa!

The swallow said she had been there many times and would lead the way. So the Doctor told Chee-Chee to pull up the anchor, and the voyage began.

THE GREAT JOURNEY

Now, for six long weeks, they sailed over the rolling seas. The swallow flew before the ship to show them the way. At night she carried a tiny lantern so that they could see her in the dark.

As they sailed farther south it became warmer. Polynesia, Chee-Chee and the crocodile loved the hot sun.

But the pig, the dog and the owl did not like the hot weather. They sat at the end of the ship in the shade of a big barrel and drank lemonade.

One evening as the sun was setting, Doctor Dolittle asked Chee-Chee to get the telescope. "Our journey is nearly over. Soon we should see the shores of Africa."

Half an hour later, they thought they could see the African coast. But it grew darker and darker and they couldn't be sure.

Suddenly a great storm hit. Thunder and lightning crashed. The wind howled. Rain poured down. The waves were so high, they splashed right over the boat.

Then they heard a big BANG! The ship stopped and rolled on its side.

"What happened?" the Doctor asked Polynesia.

"I think we're shipwrecked," said the parrot. "Tell the duck to get out and see."

Dab-Dab quickly dove under the waves. She surfaced and reported that the ship had hit a rock. There was a big hole in the bottom of the boat. The water was coming in, she said, and the ship was sinking fast.

"We must have run into Africa," the Doctor said. "I guess we'll have to swim to land."

But Chee-Chee and Gub-Gub did not know how to swim!

"Get the rope," Polynesia called. "Come here, Dab-Dab. Take the end of this rope and fly to shore. Tie it onto a palm tree and we'll hold the other end on the ship. Whoever can't swim will climb along the rope to the shore."

They all got safely to the shore, some swimming, some flying. Those who climbed on the rope carried the doctor's trunk and handbag.

"We must have run into Africa."

The rough sea beat the ship to pieces on the rock. They watched sadly as the timbers floated away.

The Doctor and the animals took shelter in a dry cave high up in the cliffs until the storm was over.

The next morning, the sun was out. They went to the sandy beach to dry themselves.

"Dear old Africa!" sighed Polynesia. "It's good to be back. Just think—tomorrow it will be one hundred sixty-nine years since I was last here! It hasn't changed a bit. Oh, there's really no place like home," she sighed. The others noticed tears in her eyes.

Suddenly Chee-Chee, the monkey, froze. "Shhh! I hear footsteps in the jungle."

They stood silently, watching as a man came out of the woods.

"What are you doing here?" the stranger asked.

"My name is John Dolittle, M.D.," said the Doctor. "I have been asked to come to Africa to cure the sick monkeys."

"You must all come to see the King," the man ordered.

"What King?" the doctor asked.

"The King of the Jolliginki," the man said. "These lands belong to him."

They gathered their baggage and followed the man through the jungle.

POLYNESIA AND THE KING

When they had walked through the thick forest, they came to the King's palace. It was a mud hut set in a wide clearing.

The King of the Jolliginki and his Queen, Ermintrude, lived there with their son, Prince Bumpo. The Prince was at the river fishing. The King and Queen sat under an umbrella before the palace door. Ermintrude snored quietly as her husband sternly watched the strangers.

"What is your business?" the King asked Doctor Dolittle. The Doctor told him why he had come to Africa.

"You may not travel through my lands," the King said. "Years ago a man came here. I was very kind to him. But he dug holes in the ground to get gold and killed elephants for their ivory tusks. He sneaked away secretly in his ship without even saying thank you. I will never let a man like that travel through Jolliginki again."

The King turned to his men. "Take away this medicine man and his animals. Lock them in my strongest prison."

The King's men locked the Doctor and his pets in a stone dungeon. It had one little window, high up in the wall, with thick bars in it.

The animals were very sad. Gub-Gub began to cry.

"Where's Polynesia?" asked the crocodile. "She isn't here."

"Are you sure?" asked the Doctor. "Polynesia! Where are you?"

"She probably escaped," grumbled the crocodile. "Just like her to sneak off when her friends are in trouble!"

"I'm not that kind of bird and you know it," the parrot said, climbing out of the Doctor's coat pocket. "I'm small enough to get through those window bars. I thought they'd put me in a cage. So I hid in the Doctor's pocket so I could help rescue you!"

"What can *you* do?" Gub-Gub said, turning up his nose. "You're just a bird!"

"I have a plan," Polynesia said. "As soon as it gets dark, I am going to creep through the window bars and fly to the palace. And then I'll find a way to make the King let us all out of prison."

That night, Polynesia slipped through the bars of the prison and flew to the palace. A window in the pantry was broken. The parrot jumped through the hole in the glass.

She heard Prince Bumpo snoring in his bed at the back of the palace. She tiptoed upstairs to the King's room, opened the door and peeped in.

"I'm small enough to get through those window bars."

The Queen was out at a dance, but the King was fast asleep in his bed.

Polynesia crept in softly and slid under the bed.

She coughed, just the way Doctor Dolittle did. Polynesia could imitate anyone!

The King half opened his eyes. "Is that you, Ermintrude?" he said sleepily.

Polynesia coughed more loudly. The King sat up, wide awake.

"Who's that?" he called.

"I am Doctor Dolittle," said the parrot, sounding just like the Doctor.

"What are you doing in my bedroom?" cried the King. "How did you get out of my prison?"

The parrot laughed, long, deep and jolly, like Doctor Dolittle.

"Stop laughing!" the King ordered. "Come here at once!"

"Foolish King," Polynesia said. "You are talking to John Dolittle, M.D., the most wonderful man on earth. You cannot see me because I have made myself invisible. I can do anything. I will make you and all your people sick if you don't let me and my animals travel through your kingdom. Send your soldiers to open the dungeon or you will have mumps before morning!"

The King trembled and was afraid. "I'll let you all go." He ran to tell the soldiers to open the prison door.

Polynesia crept downstairs and left through the pantry window.

Just coming back from the dance, the Queen spotted the parrot. When the King returned to bed, she told him. Then he realized he had been tricked. He was furious. He hurried to the prison. But he was too late. The door was open. The Doctor and his animals were gone!

THE
BRIDGE
OF APES

Queen Ermintrude had never seen her husband so angry. He yelled and screamed, calling everyone a fool. He rushed outside and woke up his army, ordering them to look for Doctor Dolittle in the jungle. He sent his servants to look, too. He even sent the Queen to help the soldiers.

The Doctor and his animals raced through the forest toward the Land of the Monkeys.

Gub-Gub's short legs soon got tired, and

the Doctor carried him, along with the trunk and his medicine bag.

The King of the Jolliginki thought the army would easily track down the Doctor. He was wrong. Chee-Chee knew the paths through the jungle even better than the King's men. The Doctor and the pets followed him to the thickest part of the forest. The monkey hid them in a big hollow tree between high rocks.

"We'd better wait here until the soldiers go back to bed," Chee-Chee whispered.

They stayed the whole night. They were safe, for no one knew of Chee-Chee's hiding place.

When daylight broke, they heard the Queen order the soldiers back. She said she was tired and there was no use looking anymore.

As soon as they left, the Doctor and the animals set off for the Land of the Monkeys. It was a long journey.

There was plenty to eat in the jungle. Chee-Chee and Polynesia knew where to find fruits and vegetables, like dates, figs, ground-nuts, ginger and yams. They drank wild orange juice sweetened with honey from the bees' nests.

At night, they slept in tents of palm leaves, on thick, soft beds of dried grass. After a while, they got used to walking and enjoyed the carefree life of travel.

The King was furious when his army returned without the Doctor, and he sent the soldiers back into the jungle to find him.

One day Chee-Chee climbed to look over the treetops. He said they were near the Land of the Monkeys.

That very evening, they met some of Chee-Chee's cousins sitting on the edge of a swamp. When they saw the famous Doctor, they cheered, waved leaves, and swung through the tree branches.

Chee-Chee's cousins wanted to help carry the Doctor's trunk and his bag. One of the bigger monkeys even carried Gub-Gub! Two rushed ahead to tell the sick monkeys that the great Doctor was on his way.

The King's men were nearby. They heard the noise and ran to where the Doctor was.

The monkey carrying Gub-Gub spotted the Army Captain hiding in the trees. He raced to the Doctor and told him to run.

Suddenly the Doctor tripped and fell in the mud. The Army Captain ran faster, sure he could catch him. But the Captain had very long ears. As he raced toward the Doctor, one of his ears got caught in a tree! The rest of the army stopped to help him.

The Doctor jumped up and ran.

"We don't have far to go now!" Chee-Chee shouted.

Suddenly they came to a steep cliff. A wide river flowed below. The Land of the Monkeys was on the other side of the river!

"Quick!" the monkey carrying Gub-Gub shouted to the other monkeys. "Make a bridge. We have only a minute. The Captain is loose from the tree and he's running like a deer. Hurry!"

When the Doctor looked back across the cliff, there was a bridge all ready for him. The

Doctor Dolittle was the last to cross.

monkeys had held hands and feet and made themselves into a bridge.

They raced across the monkey bridge. Doctor Dolittle was the last to cross. As he reached the other side, the King's men were at the edge of the cliff.

They shook their fists and yelled with rage. They were too late. The King would be furious! The Doctor and his animals were safe in the Land of the Monkeys, and the bridge was pulled across to the other side.

"You are the first human to see the famous Bridge of Apes," Chee-Chee told the Doctor.

Doctor Dolittle smiled and was very pleased.

The
Leader of
the Lions

John Dolittle was very busy. He found thousands of sick monkeys—gorillas, orangutans, chimpanzees, baboons, marmosets, and gray and red monkeys.

First he separated the sick ones from the well ones. All the healthy monkeys were ordered to come to the Doctor and be vaccinated.

For three days and nights, the monkeys came. The Doctor sat day and night, vaccinating each and every one.

He asked to have a big house made, one with lots of beds in it. He put all the sick monkeys in this house.

The Doctor needed help nursing the sick monkeys. He sent messages to the lions, leopards and antelopes for help.

The Leader of the Lions was a proud creature. He was angry when he came to the doctor's house full of sick monkeys.

"Do you dare to ask *me*, the King of Beasts, to wait on dirty monkeys that I wouldn't even eat between meals?"

The lion looked angry and ferocious. But the Doctor tried hard not to seem afraid.

"I didn't ask you to eat them," he said quietly. "And they're *not* dirty. They all had a bath this morning. It looks as though *your* coat could use a brushing." The lion growled and began to turn away.

"Let me tell you something," the Doctor said. "The day may come when the lions get sick. If you don't help these animals now, you may find yourselves all alone when *you* are in trouble."

The Doctor tried hard not to seem afraid.

The Leader of the Lions turned up his nose and walked into the jungle.

The leopards also said they wouldn't help. The antelopes were shy. They smiled and said they didn't know how to be nurses.

Poor Doctor Dolittle was frantic. Where could he get enough help to take care of thousands of sick monkeys?

When the Leader of the Lions got back to his den, his wife, the Queen Lioness, came running out to meet him. She was crying.

"One of the cubs won't eat!" she cried. "I don't know *what* to do with him."

The Leader went into his den and looked at his children. The two sweet little cubs were lying on the floor. He gulped when he saw that one seemed quite sick.

The lion returned to his wife and proudly told her what he had said to the Doctor. She got so angry, she nearly drove him out of the den.

"You did *what*?" she screamed. "All the animals from here to the Indian Ocean are talking about this wonderful man and how he can cure any sickness. And now, when we have a sick baby, you go and offend him!"

She lunged at her husband and started to pull out his hair.

"Go back at once!" she yelled. "And tell him you're sorry. Take all the other dumb lions with you and those stupid leopards and antelopes, too. Do everything the Doctor tells you. Work hard! And perhaps he will be kind enough to come and see our cub. *Hurry!*"

So the Lion Leader went back to the Doctor. "I happened to be passing by," he said. "Do you have any help yet?"

"No," said the Doctor. "I haven't. And I'm very worried."

"It's hard to get help these days," the lion said. "Animals don't seem to want to work anymore. I'll do what I can to help you. I've told the other hunting animals to come and do their share. . . . Oh, and by the way, we've got a sick cub at home. My wife's a little scared. If you are around this evening, would you take a look at him?"

"Of course," said the Doctor, who was very happy. Soon animals from the forests, mountains and plains came to help. So many came that some had to be sent away. The Doctor chose only the smarter ones to help.

The monkeys began to get well. At the end

of the week the big house was half empty. By the end of the second week, the last monkey was well.

The Doctor's work was done. He was so tired, he went to bed for three days.

THE MONKEYS' COUNCIL

Chee-Chee stood outside Doctor Dolittle's door for three days and nights. He kept everybody away until the Doctor woke up. Then Doctor Dolittle told the monkeys that he must return to Puddleby.

They were surprised and sad. They had thought the great Doctor would stay forever.

The Chief Chimpanzee asked, "Why is the good man going away? Isn't he happy here?"

*"I think we should
ask him to stay."*

But no one could answer.

The Grand Gorilla said, "I think we should ask him to stay. We can make him a new house and a bigger bed."

Chee-Chee stood up. "My friends," he said. "It is useless to ask the Doctor to stay. He owes money in Puddleby and he says he must pay it back."

"What is *money?*" they asked.

Chee-Chee told them that in the Doctor's country you couldn't get anything without money.

"You can't even eat and drink without money?" one asked.

Chee-Chee shook his head.

"What strange creatures!" the Chief Chimpanzee said.

Chee-Chee explained how the Doctor had to borrow a ship and food to come help the sick ones in the Land of the Monkeys. He told them how the storm wrecked their ship on the shores of Africa.

The monkeys sat silently. They were thinking hard.

At last, the Biggest Baboon stood and said, "We cannot let the wonderful Doctor go unless we give him a fine present to show how grateful we are to him."

They all cried out in agreement.

But what could they give?

"Fifty bags of coconuts!" one called out.

"A hundred bunches of bananas!" another suggested.

Chee-Chee shook his head. He said these would be too heavy to carry and would spoil before they reached home.

"If you really want to please him," he said,

"give him some rare animal they do not have in the menageries. You may be sure he will be kind to it."

"What are menageries?" the monkeys asked.

Chee-Chee explained that they were also called zoos and were places for people to come and look at animals in cages. The monkeys were shocked!

"It is like a prison!" one said.

They asked Chee-Chee what rare animal they should give Doctor Dolittle—one that the people of his country had not seen before.

The Major of the Marmosets suggested giving him an iguana.

"They have one in the London Zoo," Chee-Chee said.

"Do they have an okapi?" another asked.

"Yes," Chee-Chee said. "In Belgium. I saw one when I was with the organ-grinder in a big city called Antwerp."

"What about a pushmi-pullyu?" someone called out.

"No." Chee-Chee smiled. "No foreign man has *ever* seen a pushmi-pullyu. Let's give him that!"

THE RAREST ANIMAL OF ALL

Pushmi-pullyus are no longer alive. They are extinct animals, like dinosaurs. But long ago, there were a few living in the deepest jungles of Africa.

They were strange-looking creatures. They had no tail. Instead, at both ends of their body, they had a head with sharp horns! They were shy and very hard to catch. Only one half slept at a time. The other was awake and watching. There were none in zoos because not a single one had ever been caught.

The monkeys set out hunting for one for Doctor Dolittle. After going many miles, they saw strange footprints near the edge of the river. They followed the bank of the river to a place where the grass was thick and high.

"He must be in there!" one whispered excitedly.

They joined hands and made a great circle around the high grass. The pushmi-pullyu heard them coming. He tried to break through the ring of monkeys but could not do it. He sat down and waited to see what they wanted.

"Would you go away with Doctor Dolittle and put on a show?" one monkey asked.

"Certainly not!" he said, shaking both heads hard.

They explained that he would not be locked up in a zoo, but would just be shown to children and people in other parts of the world. They also told him about the Doctor's money problems.

Finally the pushmi-pullyu agreed to meet the Doctor and see what kind of a man he was.

Chee-Chee took the animal inside to the Doctor.

"What in the world is this?" the Doctor asked, as he gazed at the strange creature.

"This, Doctor," Chee-Chee said proudly, "is the pushmi-pullyu—the rarest animal of the African jungles. It is the only two-headed beast in the world! It is a gift to you from the grateful monkeys. Take it home and your fortune's made. People will pay any money to see him."

The Doctor looked at the frightened animal. "But I don't want any money," he said.

"Yes, you do," said Dab-Dab. "Don't you remember the bills we owe the butcher in Puddleby? And how are you going to get a new boat for the sailor?"

"I was going to make him one," the Doctor said.

"Where would you get the wood and the nails to make one?" Dab-Dab cried. "Besides, what are we going to live on? We'll be poorer than ever when we get back. Chee-Chee's right. Take the funny-looking thing along."

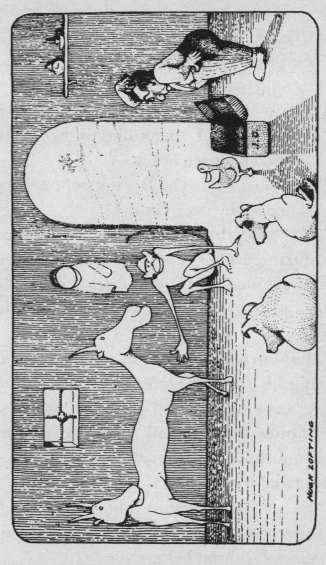

"What in the world is this?" the Doctor asked.

"Well," murmured the Doctor, "it would be nice to have a new pet. But does he really want to go abroad?"

"Yes, I'll go," said the pushmi-pullyu, who felt he could trust the Doctor. "You have been so kind to the animals here. Just please promise me that if I do not like your country you will send me back home."

"Why, of course." The Doctor smiled. "Are you related to the deer family?"

"Yes," said the pushmi-pullyu. "To the Abyssinian gazelles, and I'm related to the Asiatic chamois, on my mother's side. My father's great-grandfather was the last of the unicorns."

"Most interesting!" murmured the Doctor, rubbing his chin. He took a book from the trunk. "Let's see if Buffon says anything—"

"I notice that you talk with only one of your mouths. Can't the other head talk as well?" asked the duck.

"Oh, yes," the creature said. "But I keep the other mouth for eating. That way I can talk and eat without being rude."

When the packing was finished, the monkeys gave a big party for the Doctor with all sorts of good things to eat and drink.

After they finished eating, the Doctor stood up. "My friends," he said. "I am not good at giving dinner speeches. But I want you to know that I am very sad to leave your beautiful country. I must go because I have things to do in the Land of the Europeans. But remember, never let the flies settle on your food, and do not sleep on the ground when the rains are coming. I hope you will all live happily ever after."

The Doctor stopped speaking and sat down. All the monkeys clapped their hands for a very long time.

"Let's always remember," they said, "that Doctor Dolittle sat and ate with us, here, under the trees. He is surely the greatest of men!"

The Grand Gorilla, who had the strength of seven horses, rolled a great rock to the head of the table. "This stone will always mark the spot of our special dinner," he said.

To this day, the stone is in that spot. Monkey mothers point to it from the branches and tell their children about the good Doctor who sat there and ate with the animals in the Year of the Great Sickness.

The party ended. The Doctor and his pets started out toward the seashore. All the monkeys in the jungle followed as far as the edge of their country. They carried the Doctor's trunk and wished him a safe trip.

THE PRINCE

By the edge of the river they stopped and said goodbye. It took a long time because each of the thousands of monkeys wanted to shake John Dolittle's hand.

When the Doctor and his pets were finally alone, Polynesia warned, "We must walk lightly and talk low because we are in the Land of the Jolliginki again. If the King hears us, he will send his soldiers to catch us. I am sure he is still very angry at the trick I played on him."

"I'm wondering where we are going to find another boat to get home," the Doctor muttered. "Perhaps we'll find one that no one is using on the beach."

One day, while passing through the thickest part of the forest, Chee-Chee went ahead to look for coconuts. The Doctor and the animals got terribly lost in the thick woods. They walked around and around but could not find their way to the seashore.

When he could not find the Doctor, Chee-Chee was very upset. He climbed to the top of the tall trees, trying to see the Doctor's high hat. He waved. He shouted. He called the animals by name. It was no use. They seemed to have disappeared.

Doctor Dolittle and the animals were far from the path. They pushed through the thick jungle.

At last, they marched by mistake right into the King's backyard. The King's men ran up at once and caught them.

Polynesia flew into the garden and hid in a

tree. The Doctor and the animals were taken to the King.

"Ha, ha!" cried the King. "I knew I would catch you. This time you shall not escape. Put double locks on the prison doors. This man shall scrub my floors for the rest of his life," he laughed, pointing to the Doctor.

Doctor Dolittle and his pets were led back to prison and locked up.

"This is a great nuisance," the Doctor said. "I really must get back to Puddleby. That poor sailor will think I've stolen his ship if I don't get home soon."

The Doctor tried the hinges on the door. "They are very strong," he said sadly. Gub-Gub began to cry.

As they each found a spot on the prison floor, Polynesia sat silently in the tree in the garden palace, blinking. When Polynesia said nothing and blinked, it meant that someone had caused trouble for the Doctor and she was making a plan to set things right.

Suddenly she saw Chee-Chee swinging through the trees. He was still looking for the Doctor. Chee-Chee came to Polynesia's tree and asked what had happened.

"The Doctor and all the animals have been caught by the King's men and locked up again," whispered Polynesia. "We lost our way in the jungle and ended up in the King's garden by mistake."

"Couldn't you guide them?" Chee-Chee asked.

"Shhh! Look," Polynesia said. "There's Prince Bumpo coming into the garden! He must not see us. Don't move!"

The King's son opened the garden gate. He carried a book of fairy tales and strolled down the walk, humming a sad song. He stopped at the stone seat right under the tree where Polynesia and Chee-Chee hid. He lay down on the seat and started to read.

"I have an idea!" Polynesia whispered. "Maybe I can hypnotize him!"

"What?" Chee-Chee said.

Polynesia whispered in his ear, "When you've been hypnotized you sort of go to sleep. If someone gives you orders, you'll do whatever you've been told, even after you wake up! If I can put Prince Bumpo in a trance, I'll tell him to unlock the prison and let the Doctor out!"

Chee-Chee shrugged. "It's worth a try."

Polynesia slid quietly down the branch, closer to the Prince. Clutching a small twig, she slowly waved it in front of him, making a soft humming sound.

Prince Bumpo watched the twig slowly swinging back and forth. Soon his eyes closed. After a moment, Polynesia spoke in a quiet voice: "Bumpo, O Prince Bumpo, there is something important you must do."

He smiled gently in his sleep.

Polynesia continued: "In your father's prison is a famous Wizard. He knows many things about medicine and magic and has performed mighty deeds. Brave Bumpo, go to him when the sun has set. And don't tell any-one.

"But first," she added, "prepare a ship for him to sail. Then go and let the Great Wizard and his animals go free!"

The sleeping Prince smiled again.

The Twelfth Chapter

MEDICINE
AND
MAGIC

Very quietly, making sure no one saw her, Polynesia slipped out of the garden and across to the prison.

Gub-Gub poked his nose through the window bars, sniffing the smells from the palace kitchen. The parrot told the pig to bring the Doctor to the window.

"Listen," whispered Polynesia to the Doctor. "Prince Bumpo is going to find a ship for you. He will come here tonight to unlock the prison doors. Be ready to leave!"

"How on earth . . . ?" the Doctor began.

"Quiet! The guards are coming!" she whispered, and flew away.

Late that night the Prince came to the prison.

"O Great Wizard," he said, "I have come to set you free. I've prepared a ship for you."

Taking a bunch of copper keys from his pocket, the Prince opened the prison door's locks. The Doctor and his animals ran toward the seashore as fast as they could. Bumpo leaned against the wall of the empty dungeon, smiling.

Polynesia and Chee-Chee were waiting when they got to the beach. The pushmi-pullyu, Gub-Gub, Dab-Dab, Jip and Too-Too went onto the ship with the Doctor.

Chee-Chee, Polynesia and the crocodile waited on the shore. Africa was the land where they were born, and they had decided to stay.

The Doctor stood on the boat and looked across the water. He suddenly realized he had no one to guide them back to Puddleby.

The sea looked very big and lonesome in the moonlight. Suddenly the Doctor heard a strange whispering noise, high in the air. The animals grew silent and listened.

The noise grew louder and seemed to come closer, like a strong wind or a heavy rain. They all looked up. Streaming across the face of the moon like a huge swarm of ants were thousands of little birds. There were so many that for a while they covered the whole moon.

The birds settled on the sand and along the ship's ropes. The Doctor noticed their blue wings, white breasts and very short, feathered legs. As soon as each had found a place to sit, all was quiet and still.

John Dolittle looked around him and sighed. "I had no idea we had been in Africa so long. It will be nearly summer when we get home. These swallows are going back! Thank you, dear swallows, for waiting for us. Now we won't be afraid of losing our way upon the seas."

The Doctor stood at the side of the ship

They waved until the ship was out of sight.

and waved a final farewell to the monkey, the parrot and the crocodile.

"Pull up the anchor and set the sail!" he ordered as they followed the swallows out to sea. As the ship moved away, Chee-Chee, Polynesia and the crocodile grew very sad. Never in their lives had they known anyone they liked as much as Doctor John Dolittle.

They called goodbye to him, standing on the rocks and crying sadly. They waved until the ship was out of sight.

RED SAILS AND BLUE WINGS

ailing home, the Doctor's ship had to pass the coast of Barbary, home of the terrible Barbary pirates.

These bad pirates waited for sailors to be shipwrecked on their shores. If they saw a boat passing, they would chase it in their fast sailing ships and steal everything on it. After they took the people off, they would sink the ship. Then they would sail back to Barbary, singing songs.

They made the people they took as prisoners write home for money. If their friends sent no money, the pirates often threw the people into the sea.

One day, the Doctor and Dab-Dab walked up and down the ship for exercise. It was a beautiful, bright day. Suddenly Dab-Dab spotted the red sail of another ship a long way behind them.

"I don't like the look of that sail," Dab-Dab said. "I have a feeling it is not a friendly ship."

Lying on the deck, taking a nap, Jip began to growl and talk in his sleep.

"I smell roast beef cooking," he mumbled. "Underdone roast beef, with brown gravy."

"What's the matter with the dog?" cried the Doctor. "Is he *smelling* in his sleep, as well as talking?"

"All dogs smell in their sleep," Dab-Dab said. "The smell must be coming from that other ship over there."

"But that's ten miles away! He couldn't smell that far!"

"Yes, he could," Dab-Dab said, beginning to worry.

Still fast asleep, Jip began to growl. "I smell bad men. The worst men I ever smelled," he growled. "I smell a fight . . . six scoundrels against one brave man. I must help him! *Woof!*" he barked loudly, waking himself.

"Look!" cried Dab-Dab. "The boat is nearer now. Oh my, they are coming after us!"

"They must be the pirates of Barbary!" said Jip.

"Put more sails on our boat so we can go faster," the Doctor ordered. "Run downstairs, Jip, and get all the sails you see."

The dog returned quickly, dragging every sail he could find.

But even with the sails, the pirates' ship came closer and closer.

"This is a poor ship the Prince gave us," said the pig. "Look how near they are now! You can see the mustaches on their faces. What are we going to do?"

"They must be the pirates of Barbary!"

The Doctor asked Dab-Dab to fly up and tell the swallows about the pirates.

The swallows all came down onto the Doctor's ship. They told him to unravel several pieces of long rope and make thin strings as quickly as possible. The ends of the strings were tied to the front of the ship. The swallows took hold of the strings with their feet and flew off, pulling the boat along.

The strength of all the swallows made the Doctor's boat move swiftly.

As the red sails shrank in the distance, the animals began to laugh and dance. The pirates' red sails were being left far behind.

THE RATS' WARNING

Dragging a ship through the sea was hard work for the swallows. They sent a message to the Doctor to say that they needed to take a rest soon.

Soon the Doctor saw an island where they could rest. It had a very beautiful, high green mountain right in the middle.

When the ship had sailed safely into the bay, the Doctor said he would go onto the island to look for water because there was none left to drink on the ship. He told the animals to get off the boat and stretch their legs.

As they were getting off the boat, the Doctor noticed crowds of rats coming up from below and leaving the ship.

One big black rat stood back. He looked as if he wanted to talk to the Doctor. He crept toward the Doctor slowly.

The rat coughed nervously several times, trying to get the Doctor's attention. Finally he cleared his throat loudly. "Ahem . . . er, Doctor, you know that all ships have rats in them, don't you?"

"Yes." Doctor Dolittle nodded.

"And you have heard that rats always leave a sinking ship?"

"So I've been told," the Doctor said.

"Well, you can't blame us," said the rat. "Who *would* stay on a sinking ship if he could get off?"

"It's very natural, very natural indeed," the Doctor said. "Was there . . . anything else you wished to say?"

"Yes," said the rat. "I've come to tell you we

"And you have heard that rats always leave a sinking ship?"

are leaving this ship. But we wanted to warn you. This ship isn't safe. Before tomorrow night it will sink to the bottom of the sea."

The Doctor looked surprised. "But how do you know?"

"We always know by the tingly feeling we get in the tips of our tails," the rat explained.

"It's kind of like when your foot falls asleep. I felt it this morning. I thought it was my rheumatism, but I asked my aunt how she felt.

"Well, she said *her* tail was tingling like anything! We made up our minds to leave as soon as we got near land. Don't sail in this ship, or you'll surely be drowned. . . . Goodbye."

"Goodbye," said the Doctor. "And thank you for telling me."

The Doctor and his animals went off to look for water on the island, carrying pails and saucepans. The swallows rested.

As he climbed up the mountain, the Doctor looked around at the beautiful view. "I wonder what this island is called," he said. "It is such a pleasant place. There are a lot of birds here!"

"These are the Canary Islands," Dab-Dab said. "Don't you hear them singing?"

The Doctor listened. "Why, of course! I wonder if they can tell us where to find water."

The canaries had heard all about Doctor Dolittle. Soon they came and led him to a beautiful spring of cool, clear water.

Later, after eating and drinking, Doctor Dolittle and the animals lay in the meadows under the bright sun, listening to the canaries sing. Suddenly two swallows flew excitedly to the Doctor.

"The pirates have come into the bay," they said. "They've all gone onto your ship and are looking for things to steal. If you hurry, you can take their swifter ship and escape."

"Splendid!" said the Doctor. "Let's go!"

He called the animals together, said goodbye to the canaries and raced down to the beach.

They spotted the pirate ship with three red sails standing in the water. The pirates were below deck on the Doctor's ship, looking for loot.

Very quietly, John Dolittle and his animals crept onto the pirate ship and got ready to set sail.

THE BARBARY DRAGON

Everything would have gone well if Gub-Gub had not caught a cold eating damp sugar-cane on the island. Quietly they pulled up the anchor and moved the ship carefully into the bay. But suddenly Gub-Gub sneezed so loudly that the pirates on the other ship rushed to see what the noise was.

When they spotted the Doctor escaping on their ship, they sailed across the entrance to the bay, preventing him from heading into the open sea.

The leader of the pirates called himself Ben Ali, the Dragon. He shook his fist at the Doctor.

"Ha! Ha! You are caught, my fine friend." He laughed. "You were going to run off with my ship, eh? But you are not a good enough sailor to beat the Barbary Dragon!

"I want that duck and that pig," he continued. "We'll have pork chops and roast duck for supper tonight. And your friends will have to send me a trunkful of gold if ever you want to see your home again!"

The owl, Too-Too, whispered to the Doctor, "Be nice to him. That ship is bound to sink soon. The rats are never wrong. Keep him talking until the ship sinks under him."

"Oh, let's fight the dirty rascals!" Jip said.

"No, they have pistols and swords," the Doctor said. "I must talk to Ben Ali."

The pirates sailed nearer, laughing and yelling, "Who shall catch the pig?"

Poor Gub-Gub was terrified. The pushmi-pullyu sharpened his horns for a fight by rubbing them on the mast of the ship. Jip

"I must talk to Ben Ali."

jumped into the air, barking bad names at
Ben Ali in dog language.

Suddenly the pirates stopped laughing.
Ben Ali stared down at his feet and screeched,
"Men, the boat's leaking!"

The front of the ship went down faster and
faster, and soon the boat looked as if it was
standing on its head. The pirates clung to the
rails, masts and ropes for dear life. At last the
ship sank down to the bottom of the sea with

a dreadful gurgling sound. The six bad men bobbed about in the water, crying for help.

Some of them swam toward the shore of the island. Others tried to climb onto the Doctor's boat. Jip snapped at their noses. They were afraid to climb up the side of the ship.

Then a chorus of shrieks came from the water. *"Sharks!* The sharks are coming! Let us on before they eat us!" the pirates begged. *"Help! Help!"*

The Doctor looked up and saw the fins of the sharks all over the bay.

One great shark came near the ship. "Are you John Dolittle, the famous animal doctor?" he asked.

"Yes, that is my name," the Doctor answered.

"These pirates are bad," the shark said. "If they are trouble for you, we will gladly eat them."

"Thank you," the Doctor said. "I don't think that will be necessary. But you could do me one favor."

"Anything," the shark said.

"Don't let any of them reach the shore until I tell you. And please make Ben Ali swim over here so that I may talk to him."

"With pleasure," the shark said, and he turned and chased Ben Ali over to the Doctor.

"Listen, Ben Ali," said Doctor Dolittle, leaning over the side. "You have been a very bad man. You have killed many people. These good sharks have offered to eat you for me. But I will let you go if you promise to do as I tell you."

"What must I do?" begged the pirate.

"You must not kill any people. You must not steal. You must never sink another ship. You and your men must go to this island and grow birdseed for the canaries."

The Barbary Dragon turned pale with anger. *"Grow birdseed? Be a farmer! But I am a pirate! A sailor!"*

"You are a bad sailor. For the rest of your life you must be a peaceful farmer. The shark is awaiting my orders. Make up your mind."

"Birdseed!" Ben Ali muttered as he

looked down and saw the shark smelling his legs in the water just below. "Very well, we'll be farmers."

"Just remember," the Doctor warned. "If you do not keep your promise, I will hear of it from the canaries. I am not afraid of a cowardly pirate like you. Now go and be a good farmer and live in peace."

The Doctor turned to the big shark. Waving his hand, he signaled, "All right. Let them swim safely to the land."

Too-Too,
THE
LISTENER

Having thanked the sharks for their help, the Doctor and his friends set off on their journey home in the swift ship with three red sails.

Dab-Dab waddled over to the Doctor, smiling and full of news.

"Doctor!" she cried. "This ship is beautiful! The beds are made of silk with hundreds of pillows. There are thick carpets and silver dishes! And so many things to eat and drink! You never saw anything like it. Oh, and we found a little room down there with the door locked. Can you help us try to open it?"

So the Doctor went downstairs. The Doctor and the animals hunted for a key to the door. But nowhere could they find a key to fit the lock.

They returned to the door. Jip peered through the keyhole, but he could not see a thing. Something had been placed against the inside wall. The animals wondered what to do. Suddenly Too-Too said, "Shhh! Listen! I believe there is someone in there! I hear the noise of someone putting his hand in his pocket."

"You couldn't hear that even out here," the Doctor said.

"Pardon me, but I can," Too-Too insisted. "Almost everything makes *some* noise—if your ears are sharp enough to catch it. We owls can tell, using only one ear, the color of a kitten from the way it winks in the dark!"

"Really!" said the Doctor. "Listen again and tell me what he's doing now."

"Now he's rubbing his face with his left

"Shhh! Listen! I believe there is someone in there!"

hand. It is a small hand and a small face," Too-Too said. He listened again, hard and long.

"It is a man. He is unhappy. I distinctly heard the sound of a tear falling on his sleeve."

"Well," said the Doctor, "if the poor fellow's unhappy, we've got to get in and see what's the matter. Find me an ax and I'll chop the door down."

THE OCEAN GOSSIPS

Right away, someone found an ax, and the doctor chopped a hole in the door big enough to climb through.

It was dark inside, and at first he couldn't see anything. He struck a match.

The room was small. There was no window. In the middle of the floor sat a little boy, about eight years old, crying sadly.

The little boy was frightened to see a man before him and a bunch of animals staring through the hole in the broken door.

But as soon as he saw John Dolittle's kind face by the light of the match, he stood up and stopped crying.

"You aren't one of the pirates, are you?" he asked.

The Doctor laughed. The little boy smiled.

"You laugh like a friend," he sighed. "Not like a pirate. Do you know where my uncle is?"

"I'm afraid I don't," said the Doctor. "When did you last see him?"

"The day before yesterday," the boy said. "We were out fishing in our little boat when the pirates came and caught us. They sank our boat and brought us both onto this ship. They told my uncle he had to become a pirate like them, because he was good at sailing ships in all kinds of weather.

"But my uncle said no, he was a fisherman, and would not be a pirate. Then the leader, Ben Ali, got very angry. He said they would throw my uncle into the sea unless he obeyed.

"They sent me downstairs. I heard the noise of a fight. When they let me come up the next day, my uncle was gone. I asked where he was, but the pirates wouldn't tell me. I am afraid they threw him into the sea and drowned him," he said, crying again.

"Wait a minute," said the Doctor. "Don't cry. You must be hungry. Let's go and have tea. We'll talk this over and decide what to do. I'm sure your uncle is safe. Perhaps we can find him for you."

During tea, Dab-Dab whispered to the Doctor, "Ask the porpoises about the boy's uncle. They'll know if he drowned."

"Good idea," said the Doctor, popping a piece of bread and jam into his mouth.

"So, how did you come to be locked up in that room?" the Doctor asked the boy.

"The pirates shut me in there when they went to steal from another ship."

"What does your uncle look like?" the Doctor asked.

"He has very red hair and a picture of an anchor tattooed on his arm," the boy answered. "He is a strong man, a kind uncle and the best sailor in the South Atlantic! His fishing boat was called the *Saucy Sally*."

After tea, the boy played with the animals in the dining room. The Doctor went upstairs to look for passing porpoises.

Soon he spotted a school of them heading for Brazil. He asked them if they had seen a man with red hair and an anchor tattooed on his arm.

"The master of the *Saucy Sally*?" they asked.

"Yes," said the Doctor. "Has he been drowned?"

"His fishing boat was sunk. We saw it on the bottom of the sea. But there was no one inside," they said.

"His little nephew is on the ship with me," the Doctor explained. "He is afraid the pirates threw his uncle into the sea. Could you find out for sure whether he has been drowned or not?"

"Oh, he isn't drowned," said the porpoises. "We would know. We hear all the saltwater news. The shellfish call us the ocean gossips!

Tell the little boy we do not know where his uncle is, but he hasn't drowned in the sea."

"Thank you!" The Doctor smiled as the porpoises swam away. He ran downstairs to tell the good news to the nephew, who clapped his hands with happiness.

SMELLS

"Your uncle must now be *found*," said the Doctor.

Dab-Dab whispered, "Ask the eagles to look for the man. No living creature can see better than an eagle."

"Splendid idea," the Doctor agreed. He sent one of the swallows to find some eagles.

In an hour, the swallow returned with six different kinds of eagles: a black eagle, a bald eagle, a fish eagle, a golden eagle, an eagle vulture and a white-tailed sea eagle.

They stood on the rail of the ship like soldiers: stern, still and stiff. Their gleaming black eyes shot glances in every direction.

The Doctor stood like a general before his troops on the deck of his ship.

"A man has been lost," he said to the eagles in their language. "A fisherman with red hair and an anchor tattooed on his arm. Would you be so kind as to see if you can find him for us? This boy is his nephew." Doctor Dolittle pointed to the young boy, who did not understand a word.

Eagles do not talk very much. They looked at the boy, then turned to the Doctor. "We will do our best for you, John Dolittle." Then they flew off.

When they came back it was almost night.

"We have searched all the seas and all the countries, the islands, cities and villages in this half of the world," they said. "But we have failed. Nowhere could we see a sign of this boy's uncle. We have done our very best for you, John Dolittle."

The six great birds flapped their wings and flew home.

"Well," said Dab-Dab, "what are we going to do now? I wish Chee-Chee were here."

Jip went to the Doctor and said, "Please ask the boy if he has anything in his pockets that belonged to his uncle."

The boy showed them a gold ring his uncle had given him when the pirates were coming. He wore it around his neck on a string.

Jip smelled the ring. "That's no good. Ask him if he has anything else that belonged to his uncle."

"This was my uncle's too," the boy said, taking a big red handkerchief from his pocket.

As soon as the boy pulled it out, Jip shouted, "*Snuff,* by Jingo! Black Rappee snuff. Don't you smell it? Doctor, ask him if his uncle took snuff."

The Doctor questioned the boy. "Yes." The boy nodded. "My uncle took a lot of snuff."

"Fine!" said Jip. "Tell the boy I'll find his uncle in less than a week. Let us go upstairs and see which way the wind is blowing."

"But it's dark now," the Doctor said.

"I don't need any light to look for a man who smells of Black Rappee snuff," said Jip as he climbed the stairs. "Now, let's see which way the wind is blowing. Wind is very important in long-distance smelling. A nice, steady, damp breeze is the best. . . . Ha! This wind is from the north."

Jip went to the front of the ship and smelled the wind.

"Tar, Spanish onions, kerosene, wet raincoats, crushed laurel leaves, foxes . . . hundreds of them," he muttered, his eyes closed.

"Can you really smell those different things?" the Doctor asked.

"Of course!"

Jip shut his eyes more tightly and poked

"Do you smell any parsnips?" asked Gub-Gub.

his nose straight into the air, sniffing hard with his mouth half open.

"Do you smell any parsnips?" asked Gub-Gub.

"No," snapped Jip. "All you think about is food. No parsnips and no snuff. We must wait until the wind changes to the south."

"I think you're a fake, Jip!" laughed Gub-Gub.

"You're going to get a bite on the nose in a minute!" Jip said angrily.

"Stop quarreling!" cried the Doctor. "Life's too short. Tell me, Jip, where do you think those smells are coming from?"

"From Devon and Wales, most of them," Jip said.

"My, my. That's really quite remarkable. I must make a note of that for my new book. Let's go down to supper. I'm hungry."

"So am I," said Gub-Gub.

THE ROCK

Up they got early the next morning, and saw that the sun was shining brightly. The wind blew from the south.

Jip smelled the south wind for half an hour. He came to the Doctor, shaking his head.

"I smell no snuff yet. We must wait until the wind changes to the east."

But even when the east wind came at three o'clock that afternoon, Jip could not smell the snuff.

The little boy was very disappointed and began to cry again.

"Tell him when the wind changes to the west, I will find his uncle," Jip told the Doctor.

Three days passed before the west wind came. It came early on a Friday morning, just as it was getting light. A fine, rainy mist lay like a thin fog on the sea. The wind was soft, warm and wet.

Jip awoke, ran upstairs and poked his nose into the air. He rushed to wake up the Doctor.

"I've got it!" he cried. "Doctor! Doctor!

"I've got it!" he cried.

Wake up. The wind is from the west and it smells of snuff! Start the ship. Quick!"

The Doctor tumbled out of bed. He went to the rudder to steer the ship.

"I'll go to the front and you watch my nose," Jip said. "Whichever way I point it, turn the ship the same way. The man cannot be far away. The smell is very strong!"

All morning Jip stood at the front of the ship, sniffing the wind and pointing the way for the Doctor to steer.

At lunchtime, Jip asked Dab-Dab to tell the Doctor he was worried and needed to speak to him. The Doctor came from the other end of the ship.

"The boy's uncle is starving," Jip said. "We must go as fast as we can."

"How do you know he is starving?" asked the Doctor.

"Because there is no other smell in the west wind but snuff. No food. Not even drinking water. We are getting nearer all the time because the smell grows stronger every minute."

All morning Jip stood at the front of the ship, sniffing the wind.

"All right," said the Doctor. He sent Dab-Dab to ask the swallows to pull the ship faster. The little birds came immediately and harnessed themselves to the ship. The boat raced so quickly that the fish were forced to jump out of the way.

Hour after hour went by. The ship went

rushing over the same flat sea with no land in sight.

The animals became silent and anxious. The little boy grew sad. Jip's face had a worried frown on it.

At last, late in the afternoon, Too-Too, perched on the tip of the mast, cried out, "Jip! I see a great rock in front of us. Out where the sky and water meet. Is the smell coming from there?"

"Yes!" Jip called back. "That's it."

When they got nearer, they saw that the rock was as large as a big field.

The Doctor sailed the ship around the rock. They didn't see a single living thing on it.

They stood still, listening for any sound. The only noise was the gentle lapping of waves against the side of the ship.

They called and yelled until their voices were hoarse.

The little boy burst into tears. "I'm afraid I will never see my uncle again!"

But Jip called to the Doctor, "He must be

there. The smell goes no farther. Sail the ship close to the rock and let me jump out on it."

The Doctor brought the ship as close as he could. He let the anchor down. He and Jip jumped from the ship to the rock.

Jip put his nose close to the ground. He began to run all over the place, zigzagging and twisting. The Doctor ran close behind him until he was out of breath.

At last Jip barked and sat down. The Doctor ran to him and found the dog staring into a big, deep hole in the middle of the rock!

"The boy's uncle is down there," Jip said quietly. "No wonder the eagles couldn't find him."

The Doctor crawled into the hole. It seemed to be a kind of cave or tunnel, and it ran a long way underground. He struck a match and started along the dark passage with Jip following behind.

The passage ended. The Doctor found himself in a tiny room with rock walls.

And there, in the middle of the room, his head resting on his arms, lay a man with very red hair. It was the boy's uncle, and he was fast asleep!

Jip sniffed the ground beside him. The Doctor stooped and picked up an enormous snuffbox, full of Black Rappee!

THE FISHERMAN'S TOWN

Gently the Doctor woke the man up.

But just at that moment, the match went out. The man thought Doctor Dolittle was Ben Ali, the bad pirate. He began punching at him in the dark.

Doctor Dolittle told the man who he was and that he had his nephew on his ship. The man was very grateful and said he was sorry he had punched the Doctor. He gave the Doctor a pinch of snuff.

He told the Doctor that the Barbary

Dragon had left him on the rock because he would not become a pirate. He slept in this hole in the ground because there was no place above to keep warm.

"For four days I have had nothing to eat or drink. I have lived on snuff," he said.

"What did I tell you?" Jip barked.

They struck some more matches and made their way through the passage to the daylight. The Doctor hurried the man onto the ship to give him some food.

The animals and the little boy cheered when they saw Jip and the Doctor heading toward the ship with the red-haired man.

Jip was very proud of himself, and happy to reunite the boy and his uncle. He tried not to be conceited.

When Dab-Dab said, "Jip, I had no idea you were so clever!" he just tossed his head. "That's nothing special," he said. "But it takes a dog to find a man. Birds are no good for that."

The Doctor asked the red-haired fisherman where home was. When the fisherman told him, the Doctor asked the swallows to guide the ship there first.

When they came to the land the man was from, they saw a little fishing town at the foot of a rocky mountain. The man showed them the house where he lived.

While they were letting down the anchor, the little boy's mother (who was the man's sister) came running to the shore, laughing and crying at the same time. She had sat on the hill for twenty days, waiting for them to return.

The fisherman and his sister begged the Doctor to spend a few days with them. So John Dolittle and his animals spent the weekend in the fishing village.

All the little boys who lived in the village went down to the beach and pointed to the great ship anchored there.

"That was the pirate ship of Ben Ali! The old gentleman with the high hat took the ship away from the Barbary Dragon and made him into a farmer!"

For two and a half days the Doctor stayed

in the little town. People asked him to teas, luncheons, dinners and parties. The ladies sent him boxes of flowers and candies. And every night, the village band played tunes under his window.

Finally the Doctor said, "Good people, I thank you for your kindness. But I really must be going home now."

Just as the Doctor was about to leave, the Mayor of the town came down the street. He stopped before the house where the Doctor was staying. Everybody in the village gathered around to watch.

Six pageboys blew on trumpets. The Doctor stood with the Mayor.

"Doctor John Dolittle," the Mayor said. "It is a great pleasure for me to present to the man who rid the seas of the Dragon of Barbary this little token from the grateful people of our worthy town."

The Mayor handed the Doctor a beautiful watch with real diamonds on the back!

Then the Mayor pulled a larger parcel from his pocket. "Where is the dog?"

Everyone looked for Jip. Dab-Dab found him in the village stableyard, where all the dogs of the countryside stood around him, speechless with admiration and respect.

Jip went to the Doctor's side. The Mayor opened the large parcel. Inside was a dog collar made of solid gold! The Mayor bent down and put it around Jip's neck. Written on the collar in big letters were the words: JIP—THE CLEVEREST DOG IN THE WORLD.

The crowd went to the beach to see them off. The red-haired fisherman, his sister, and the little boy thanked the Doctor and his dog over and over again.

Finally the great, swift ship with the red sails turned toward Puddleby. It sailed out to sea as the village band played music on the shore.

HOME
AGAIN

March's winds had come and gone, April's showers were over, and May's buds had opened into flowers. The June sun shined brightly when John Dolittle finally returned to his own country.

But the Doctor did not go right back to Puddleby. First he traveled through the land with the pushmi-pullyu in a gypsy wagon, stopping at every county fair.

With the acrobats on one side and the puppet shows on the other, they hung out a big sign that read: COME AND SEE THE MARVELOUS TWO-HEADED ANIMAL FROM THE JUNGLES OF AFRICA. ADMISSION: SIXPENCE.

The pushmi-pullyu stayed in the wagon while the other animals rested underneath. The Doctor sat in front taking the money as people went in. Dab-Dab scolded him for letting the children in for nothing when she wasn't looking.

Zookeepers and circus men asked the Doctor to sell them the strange creature, offering lots of money for him.

But the Doctor shook his head. "No. The pushmi-pullyu is free to come and go, like you and me."

At first, being part of a circus was interesting. But after a few weeks, the Doctor and the animals longed to go home.

Since so many people came to the little wagon and paid the sixpence to go inside, the Doctor was soon able to give up being a showman.

And finally he returned to Puddleby-on-

The Doctor sat in front.

the-Marsh. He was a rich man, happy to be home.

The old, lame horse in the stable welcomed him. The swallows had already returned, built their nests under the eaves and had babies. Dab-Dab was glad to get back to the house, even though there were cobwebs and a lot of dusting to be done.

Jip went to show his solid gold collar to the conceited collie next door. Gub-Gub dug up the horseradish, which had grown to three feet by the garden wall while they were away!

The Doctor bought the kind sailor who had lent him the boat *two* new ships, as well as a rubber doll for his baby. He paid the grocer and bought another piano for the white mice to live in.

Even when the Doctor had filled his old money box, he had so much left over, he had to get three more!

"Money is a terrible nuisance," he said. "But it's nice not to have to worry."

When winter came again, snow flew against the kitchen window. The Doctor and his animals would sit around the big fire, and he would read aloud from his books.

But far away in Africa, the monkeys chattered about the their dear friend. "I wonder what the good man's doing now," they said to each other. "Do you think he will ever come back?"

Polynesia would squawk out from the vines, "I think he will. I guess he will. I hope he will!"

The crocodile would grunt at them from the black mud of the river. "I'm *sure* he will! Now go to sleep!"

THE END

ABOUT THE AUTHOR

Hugh Lofting was born in Maidenhead, England, in 1886 and was educated at home with his brothers and sister until he was eight. He studied engineering in London and at the Massachusetts Institute of Technology. After his marriage in 1912 he settled in the United States.

During World War I he left his job as a civil engineer, was commissioned a lieutenant in the Irish Guards, and found that writing illustrated letters to his children eased the strain of war. "There seemed to be very little to write to youngsters from the front; the news was either too horrible or too dull. One thing that kept forcing itself more and more upon my attention was the very considerable part the animals were playing in the war. That was the beginning of an idea: an eccentric country physician with a bent for natural history and a great love of pets . . ."

These letters became *The Story of Doctor Dolittle,* published in 1920. Children all over the world have read this book and the eleven that followed, for they have been translated into almost every language. *The Voyages of Doctor Dolittle* won the Newbery Medal in 1923. Drawing from the twelve Doctor Dolittle volumes, Hugh Lofting's sister-in-law, Olga

Fricker, later compiled *Doctor Dolittle: A Treasury,* which was published by Dell in 1986 as a Yearling Classic.

Hugh Lofting died in 1947 at his home in Topanga, California.